AF606918

KACEY MUSGRAVES

Tammy Gagne

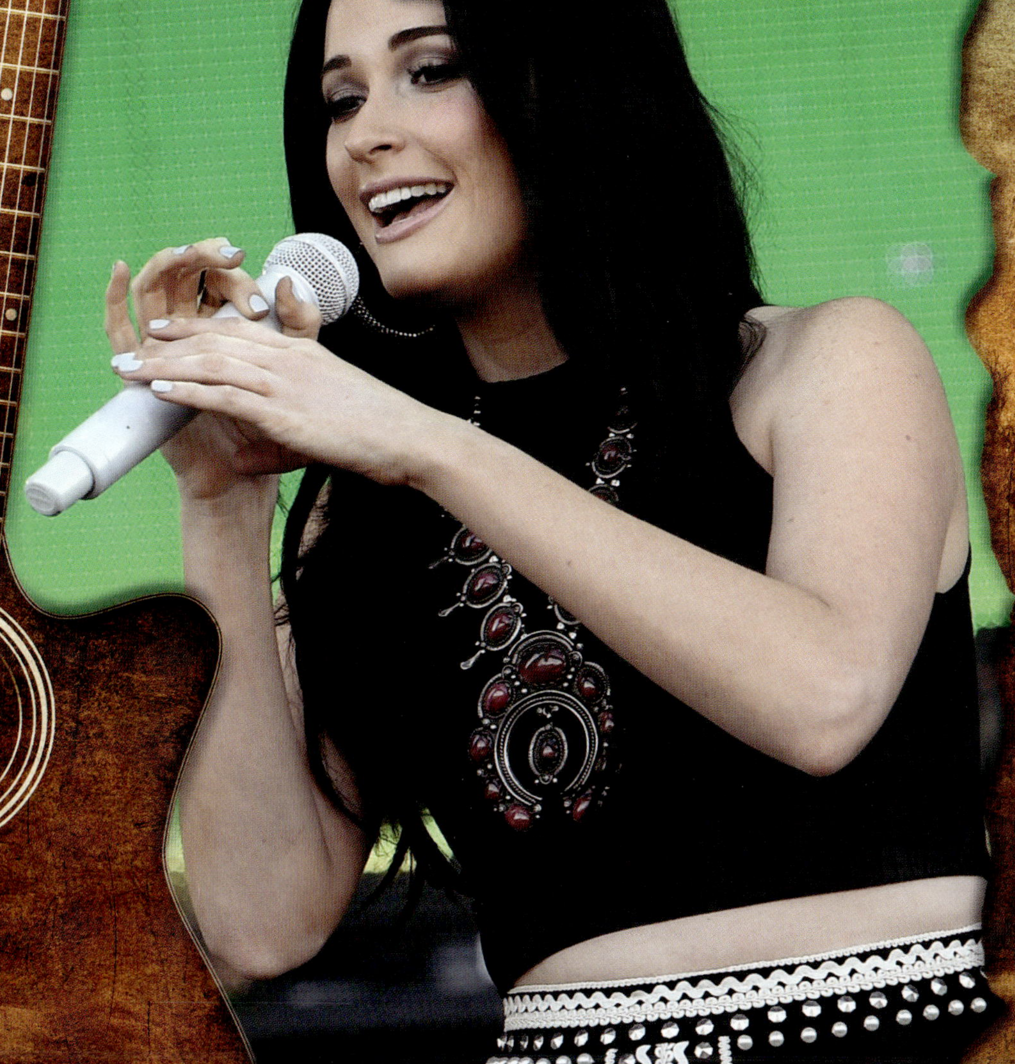

Mitchell Lane
PUBLISHERS
2001 SW 31st Avenue
Hallandale, FL 33009
www.mitchelllane.com

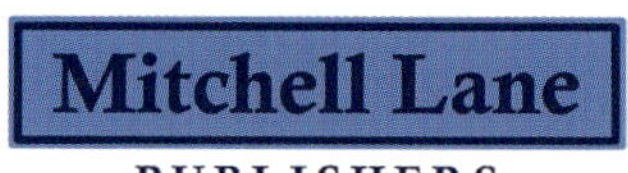

Printing 1 2 3 4 5 6 7 8 9

Brett Eldridge
Chris Stapleton
Dierks Bentley

Eric Church
Jake Owen
Kacey Musgraves

Designer: Sharon Beck
Editor: Jim Whiting

Library of Congress Cataloging-in-Publication Data
Names: Gagne, Tammy.
Title: Kacey Musgraves / by Tammy Gagne.
Description: Hallandale, FL : Mitchell Lane Publishers, [2018] | Series: Country's newest stars | Includes index.
Identifiers: LCCN 2017046725 | ISBN 9781680201604 (library bound)
Subjects: LCSH: Musgraves, Kacey—Juvenile literature. | Country musicians—United States—Biography—Juvenile literature.
Classification: LCC ML3930.M94 G34 2018 | DDC 782.421642092 [B] —dc23
LC record available at https://lccn.loc.gov/2017046725

eBook ISBN: 9-781-68020-161-1

ABOUT THE AUTHOR: Tammy Gagne has written more than 200 books for both adults and children. Her recent titles include several books about country music artists, including *Dierks Bentley* and *Brett Eldredge*. She resides in northern New England with her husband and son.

PUBLISHER'S NOTE: The following story has been thoroughly researched and to the best of our knowledge represents a true story. While every possible effort has been made to ensure accuracy, the publisher will not assume liability for damages caused by inaccuracies in the data and makes no warranty on the accuracy of the information contained herein. This story has not been authorized or endorsed by Kacey Musgraves.

PHOTO CREDITS: Design elements: (vintage paper guitar lake scene)—RhaStudio/iStock/Getty Images Plus, (star)—Andre_/DigitalVision Vectors/Getty Images, (abstract grunge)—Chen Ping-hung/Hemera/Getty Images Plus, (Contents background)—bobvidler/DigitalVision Vectors, (back matter banner)— fatmayilmaz/DigitalVision Vectors; cover, pp. 1, 10, 13, 15, 17, 25, 27—Rick Diamond/Staff/Getty Images Entertainment; p. 5—BruceC007/cc by-sa 4.0; p. 7—Rusty Russell/Stringer/Getty Images Entertainment; p. 8—Larry Busacca/Staff/Getty Images Entertainment; p. 19—Michael Loccisano/Staff/Getty Images Entertainment; p. 21—Splash News/Alamy Stock Photo; p. 22—Larry Philpot/cc-by-sa 2.0; p. 23—Mike Windle/Staff/Getty Images Entertainment; p. 26—Frazer Harrison/Staff/Getty Images Entertainment.

CONTENTS

1 Following Her Arrow

Hailey strolled into the guitar shop, just like she had done every Thursday evening for the last six months. She took lessons in the back room from Mrs. Fenderson, the store's owner. The shop itself was pristine with shiny new guitars lining the walls from floor to ceiling on three sides. The back wall was reserved for vintage instruments. Some of them cost more than the most expensive new guitars. Hailey nodded to her teacher as she passed the cash register and headed toward the door with the sign "Employees Only." In a few minutes, Mrs. Fenderson would lock the outside door and join her to begin their lesson.

The back room was filled with boxes, spare cords, and instruments on layaway. One older Gibson guitar hung on the wall above the chaos, as if it were too special to spend time in such a dreadful place. It seemed to have

Kacey had quickly become one of Hailey's favorite country music artists. She loved the sound of her voice . . .

Kacey has been playing the guitar since she was a young teen. Performing in front of large audiences comes naturally to her.

been there since Hailey first started coming. She always thought it was a shame that no one had played such a beautiful instrument for so long. She often wondered if the buyer would ever finish paying it off—or if that person had simply forgotten about it. It reminded her of the guitar she had seen Kacey Musgraves playing.

Kacey had quickly become one of Hailey's favorite country music artists. She loved the sound of her voice

Hailey could hardly believe she was the proud new owner of the Gibson.

and the way she played the guitar. And she especially admired Kacey for writing her own songs. Hailey hoped that one day she too could write music and play it for other people. Her guitar wasn't nearly as nice as the ones Kacey played. But it was the best her family could afford. And she delighted in playing every chord she had learned on it.

As she was tuning her guitar, Hailey heard her mother's voice coming from the store. Before she had time to wonder what her mother was doing there, Mrs. Fenderson led her through the doorway. Her mother held a piece of paper with "PAID" stamped across the top in red ink.

"Thank you so much for holding it for so long," her mother said as Mrs. Fenderson retrieved the vintage Gibson.

"It was my pleasure," Mrs. Fenderson replied. Then she asked Hailey, "Would you like to play a song for your mother on your new guitar before tonight's lesson?"

Hailey could hardly believe she was the proud new owner of the Gibson. She was still far from being able to play songs like her idol did. But she was determined to make her mother proud as she began strumming her beautiful new instrument.

A Star in the Making

Kacey Musgraves began her rise to fame in 2007 as a contestant on the fifth season of USA Network's reality television show *Nashville Star*. The singing competition helped aspiring country singers find an audience. The winner of each season received a record deal. Although Kacey, then just 18 years old, only came in seventh in the competition, she has become one of the most successful artists from the popular show.

Kacey performs during the premiere episode of *Nashville Star* on January 11, 2007 in Nashville, Tennessee.

Her first mainstream album, *Same Trailer Different Park*, would rise to number one on Billboard's Top Country Albums chart after its release in 2013. She also won Song of the Year at the Country Music Association Awards the following year for "Follow Your Arrow." Kacey says the song started out as a poem. She wrote it for a friend who was leaving the country to study in Paris, France. After buying her friend an arrow necklace as a going-away gift, Kacey became inspired. The poem turned into a song about the importance of embracing one's true self.

Kacey (left) and Brandy Clark won Song of the Year for "Follow Your Arrow" at the 48th annual CMA Awards in 2014.

"Follow Your Arrow" is not a typical country music song. Kacey sang of open-mindedness about such things as same-sex relationships and marijuana. Few country music artists had ever addressed these topics. Not all of Kacey's fans loved the tune. It only reached number 43 on the Billboard Country Airplay chart. Even this was significant, though. The song was the lowest charting single to win Song of the Year. In 2014, *Rolling Stone* rated the song 39th on its list of the 100 greatest country songs of all time. And Kacey and her co-writer Brandy Clark became two of only 14 female songwriters to win the prestigious award.

2 The Young Songwriter

Kacey Lee Musgraves didn't grow up in a trailer park. But she did live in one when she was born in Golden, Texas on August 21, 1988. Her parents, Craig and Karen, run a print shop that creates graphic designs for T-shirts and other merchandise. Kacey also has a younger sister named Kelly, who often tours with the country star. The two girls grew up with her grandmother living next door.

Creativity seems to be passed down through the women in Kacey's family, although they all have different interests. Kacey's grandmother makes all-natural scented soaps. In addition to running the print shop, Kacey's mother is a visual artist who paints and makes sculptures from objects such as driftwood. And Kacey's sister has an Etsy store where she sells her hand-sewn items. Kelly has also been Kacey's personal professional photographer since the beginning of her career.

Creativity seems to be passed down through the women in Kacey's family, although they all have different interests.

Kacey (left) and Kelly remain close as adults. Sometimes Kelly even goes on tour with her older sister.

Although she isn't a singer herself, Karen taught her daughter to sing harmony when she was a child. Kacey began singing when she was just 8 years old. When LeAnn Rimes released her hit song "Blue," Kacey was one of many girls who wanted to learn to yodel like the young country star. With the support of her family, Kacey entered numerous talent shows in East Texas.

In addition to the guitar, DeFoore taught Kacey to play the mandolin and the banjo.

By the time she was 13, Kacey wanted to learn something new—how to play the guitar. Her parents helped by signing her up for lessons with a local musician named John DeFoore. He was also Miranda Lambert's guitar teacher. The two young women became friends as teens. In addition to the guitar, DeFoore taught Kacey to play the mandolin and the banjo. Many music teachers focus on showing their students how to play chords and scales. But DeFoore also required his students to write songs as well.

Writing songs wasn't a new thing for Kacey, even at this young age. She

Mandolin

Kacey wrote more and more as she moved through her teen years.

had actually written her first tune at the age of nine. It was called "Notice Me." Like "Follow Your Arrow," this song began as a poem. Her mother still has the copy of the lyrics. It would take many years for Kacey to make it big in the world of country music. But now "Notice Me" seems like it was predicting the future.

Kacey wrote more and more as she moved through her teen years. Many girls who go through painful romantic breakups turn to their friends for support. Kacey turned to songwriting instead. Being an aspiring country music singer wasn't always easy for her as an adolescent. She often felt that the music she played and the costumes she wore made her seem uncool to other people her age. But now she sees that even those experiences offered inspiration for songwriting. She still draws on them today.

Pursuing Her Dream

Kacey describes herself as a "not-so-great" student in high school. As her graduation approached in 2006, she knew that college wasn't for her. Her parents couldn't really afford to pay for classes she didn't want to take. Instead, she opted to move to Texas's capital city of Austin to pursue a career in music.

Miranda Lambert had gotten her big break on *Nashville Star* three years earlier. In 2007, Kacey followed in the famous singer's footsteps yet again by landing a spot in the competition. But being eliminated in the third week and coming in seventh didn't seem like much of a victory. After her exit from the contest, Kacey had to take odd jobs to get by. One of them involved working at children's birthday parties as a singing Cinderella and the Disney Channel character Hannah Montana.

While Kacey was living in Austin, she met fellow Texas singer-songwriter Radney Foster. He convinced her to move to Nashville in 2008.

She never gave up on her dream, though. While Kacey was living in Austin, she met fellow Texas singer-songwriter Radney Foster. He convinced her to move to Nashville in 2008. He told her that living in the center of the country music world offered the biggest chance of success. He would later invite her to sing backup vocals for him on his tour.

Radney Foster

She still hadn't become a country star yet. But the jobs were getting better, and she was making connections. Foster introduced her to many people in the music business. She credits him as someone she has to thank for her success today. "He totally paid it forward," she told the *Washington Post* in 2013.

3 Recording and Touring

Many successful music artists have one opportunity that is often called their big break. It is usually a record deal or an invitation to open for an established musician. For Kacey, both of these things happened in 2012. Mercury Records offered her a record deal, and she received the opportunity to open for Lady Antebellum on the group's Own the Night Tour.

Even before Kacey recorded *Same Trailer Different Park*, she was writing hit songs. When Miranda Lambert married Blake Shelton in 2011, she invited Kacey to the wedding. At the rehearsal dinner, Miranda asked Kacey about "Mama's Broken Heart," a song that Kacey had co-written with Shane McAnally and Brandy Clark. She wanted to record it. Kacey agreed, on the condition that she could sing the harmonies. The song became Miranda's 14th top-30 single.

Even before Kacey recorded *Same Trailer Different Park*, she was writing hit songs.

Kacey (right) has been friends with fellow country artist Miranda Lambert since they were kids. Kacey wrote Miranda's hit song "Mama's Broken Heart."

Kacey was making a name for herself in the world of country music. She was also earning a reputation for telling it like it is. Her fans responded to her no-nonsense style of songwriting. Although some of her songs began as poems, she points out that lyrics don't need to sound poetic. She often gets inspired when a certain phrase just pops into her head. She has said she wants her songs to sound like simple conversations. Perhaps it is that authenticity that country music fans respond to when they hear her music.

Kacey thinks that too many songwriters focus their energy on what they think people want to hear instead of what they have to say. She especially dislikes the overused premise in country songs of the bitter woman who has been wronged. She wants to sing about things other than smashing things out of anger.

Kacey thinks that too many songwriters focus their energy on what they think people want to hear instead of what they have to say.

As Kacey was touring with Lady Antebellum in the United Kingdom, "Undermine," a song she had co-written with Trent Dabbs about a year earlier, was featured on the hit ABC drama *Nashville*. It was actually recorded by the stars of the show, Hayden Panettiere and Charles Esten. But it was another entry on Kacey's growing résumé.

Differences Can Be Good

Among the many fans who embraced Kacey's new album was pop superstar Katy Perry. After she heard one of the album's songs, "Merry Go 'Round," Katy even tweeted a link to her millions of followers so they could easily pre-order *Same Trailer Different Park*. Shortly after Katy's tweet, Kacey's own Twitter following jumped sky-high.

Although their music couldn't be more different, Kacey and Katy have something important in common.

Neither one follows the unspoken rules of what should and shouldn't be the subject of a song. Katy was already known for speaking her mind through her music. It made sense that she would enjoy having some company in her outspokenness.

Although she focuses on writing country songs, Kacey has varied tastes in music. Her influences include singer-songwriter John Prine, oldies favorite The Beach Boys, and alternative rock group Weezer. And of course she is a big Katy Perry fan.

Kacey (left) performed with Katy Perry in 2014 during CMT Crossroads at Sony Pictures Studios.

In 2013, Kacey teamed up with Katy and several other female artists for Katy's We Can Survive concert in Los Angeles. Sara Bareilles, Ellie Goulding, and Tegan & Sara also performed at the benefit show for young women fighting breast cancer. The response from fans was so strong that Katy invited Kacey to accompany her on her Prismatic World Tour in 2014. In addition to being a country music star, Kacey would now be crossing the boundary between the two genres to perform for pop music audiences.

4 Doing Things Her Way

Kacey released her second album, *Pageant Material*, in 2015. Like *Same Trailer Different Park*, it rose to the top spot on Billboard's Top Country Albums chart. Shortly after the album's release, Kacey revealed that in addition to competing as a singer in talent shows, she had also been a pageant contestant as a child. She entered the Little Miss Tater Tot Pageant when she was just three years old. It was her first and only beauty pageant. Even then, though, her personality came through. A video of her appearance shows the announcer stating that young Kacey enjoyed singing and dancing but that she did not like bedtime or the word *no*.

Like her first record, *Pageant Material* was filled with catchy tunes and bold lyrics. Kacey also hadn't lost her talent for controversy. "Biscuits" in particular did not sit well with everyone at her record label. Some people

Kacey revealed that in addition to competing as a singer in talent shows, she had also been a pageant contestant as a child.

wanted her to change one word in the song that they worried would offend listeners. Kacey refused. She told *Rolling Stone*, "People are so worried about offending that they water down everything. Come to a show, and that's the line everyone loves. Don't take that away from me!"

Kacey enjoys performing live for her fans. A big part of what draws them to her music is that she tells it like it is in her songs.

> **Kacey thinks that country music should be about real life.**

People in the country music industry keep telling Kacey about the rules she should follow to be successful. But she doesn't see things their way. She doesn't want to do what everyone else has done to sell records or concert tickets.

Kacey thinks that country music should be about real life. She doesn't see herself as a rebel. Instead, she describes herself as a millennial who is writing about the world in which she lives today. She realizes that this goes against the grain of country music. But it's that grain she hopes to help change with her music.

Getting Involved

Kacey has never forgotten her roots even as she has become one of the biggest stars in country music. She has said that she loves that she grew up in such a small town (Golden has a population of just 398). She thinks that living in a small town keeps people grounded. When everyone knows everyone else, people tend to be nicer to one another.

In September, 2015, Kacey performed a benefit concert in Mineola, the next town over from Golden. The proceeds from her Hometown Hang, as it was called, went to local school art and music programs. She thinks that the arts are often overlooked as important parts of education, and she wants to change that.

Also that September, Kacey performed at the 30th anniversary of Farm Aid, a benefit concert led by legendary country music artist Willie Nelson. The charity

In 2015, Kacey lent her talents to an important cause—Farm Aid 30. The charity event helps people who make their living on family farms.

helps strengthen family farms in the United States. Nelson had long been one of Kacey's country music idols. She loves his sense of humor and the honesty he brings to his own songwriting. She included a cover of Nelson's song "Are You Sure" as a hidden track on *Pageant Material*. And Nelson sang on the re-recording with Kacey, making it a very special duet for her.

Following the 2016 Orlando, Florida gay nightclub shootings that took the lives of 49 people, Kacey took part in another special project. She joined 23 fellow music artists to record a song called "Hands." Adam Lambert, Gwen Stefani, and Meghan Trainor were just a few of the other musicians who took part in the project. They hoped the song, which is a ballad about kindness, would help the 53 survivors and others know they were not alone. Proceeds went to the help the families affected by this

Willie Nelson

tragedy with medical expenses, counseling, and education.

After high school, a close friend of Kacey confided to her that he was gay. She was in fact the first person he told. She remembers him telling her that he didn't feel like he could be himself around others. Now Kacey hopes her music will help make a difference for people who are struggling with the same situation. She is inspired by the idea of making young people like her friend feel more accepted.

After high school, a close friend of Kacey confided to her that he was gay. She was in fact the first person he told.

Kacey performed alongside Joe Walsh, Chris Stapleton, James Taylor, and Vince Gill during All For The Hall Los Angeles. The concert benefitted educational programs at the Country Music Hall of Fame and Museum.

Life, Love, and New Music

Being a country superstar doesn't leave much time for recreation. But Kacey tries to make the most of her time off. She is just as down-to-earth off the stage as she is on it. She enjoys watching Netflix. One of her favorite shows is *The Unbreakable Kimmy Schmidt*. She also enjoys relaxing with friends in her inflatable hot tub. She has joked that buying it was one of the most "redneck things" she's ever done.

Kacey enjoys staying fit. But it can be challenging when she spends so much time on a tour bus. She does yoga whenever she can. And she always takes along a bicycle. She likes riding around in the cities and towns where the bus stops. She often gets coffee, does some shopping, or has her nails done while she is out on those two-wheeled excursions.

One of Kacey's best friends is her dog Pearl. She rescued the Jack Russell/pit bull mix, who is all white with

Being a country superstar doesn't leave much time for recreation. But Kacey tries to make the most of her time off.

a single brown patch surrounding her left eye. Sometimes Kacey takes the dog on the road with her. In 2011, Pearl was hit by a car, leaving her fighting for life. She survived. But she lost one of her legs as a result.

Kacey also managed to find time for romance. She began dating fellow country singer-songwriter Ruston Kelly in the summer of 2016. Ruston has written songs for such country greats as Kenny Chesney and Tim McGraw. Like Kacey, Ruston has a musical style that crosses genres. He has toured with the rock band The Lumineers.

In 2016, she brought Ruston home for Christmas. They spent Christmas Eve watching home movies that her

Kacey attended the 50th annual CMA Awards with fellow country star Ruston Kelly. Little did she know then that they would be married less than a year later.

family had recorded while she was growing up. Then Ruston got down on one knee and presented Kacey with a little pink velvet box as he asked her to marry him. She says that in that moment she finally understood what people mean when they say they "just know" when something is right. She immediately said "Yes!" They were married the following October.

Album Number Four

Kacey's fans are eagerly looking forward to her next album. But she isn't rushing to put it out. After being on the road for so long, she needed to take a break from touring. She has also cut back on performing in general. This time away from the stage allows her to write new songs. It is difficult to do that when she has a busy show schedule.

Kacey sees *Same Trailer Different Park* and *Pageant Material* as similar in style. She wants her next album to be different. She has said she is considering such genres as reggae and surf-rock. She especially likes the idea of making a concept album, which is a record with a certain theme.

She released a holiday album in 2016 called *A Very Kacey Christmas*. It features both classic holiday songs and music she wrote. Reviewers praised the record

Kacey signed copies of her album *A Very Kacey Christmas* for fans at Ernest Tubb Record Shop in Nashville in 2016.

for its diversity. Kacey moved easily from a Latin sound on "Feliz Navidad" to a Hawaiian beat on "Mele Kalikimaka." She performed some of the songs from the album on ABC's *CMA Country Christmas* special.

Kacey also teamed up with the Zac Brown Band in 2017 to record a cover of John Prine's song "All the Best" on the band's album *Welcome Home*. Although Kacey only sang harmonies, she enjoyed taking part in the project. Like Kacey, Brown holds a deep respect for John Prine as an artist.

Kacey hasn't decided what type of music she wants to record next, but she finds that uncertainty exciting. After performing with Loretta Lynn at the CMA Awards in 2014, she told *Rolling Stone*, "At this point I don't have a bucket list anymore. I'm just along for the ride."

1988 Kacey Lee Musgraves is born on August 21.
2001 She starts guitar lessons.
2007 Kacey appears on the CMT show *Nashville Star*, placing seventh in the competition.
2008 She moves to Nashville to pursue a career in country music.
2012 After working as a songwriter, Kacey lands a record deal with Mercury Records.
2013 Kacey performs with several other artists at Katy Perry's We Can Survive concert in Los Angeles, a charity event for young women fighting breast cancer.
2014 Kacey's song "Follow Your Arrow" wins Song of the Year at the CMAs. She joins Katy Perry's Prismatic World Tour.
2016 Kacey becomes engaged to fellow songwriter Ruston Kelly.
2017 Kacey marries Ruston Kelly in October.

2013 *Same Trailer Different Park*
2015 *Pageant Material*
2016 *A Very Kacey Christmas*

On the Internet

Country Music Television, Kacey Musgraves
http://www.cmt.com/artists/kacey-musgraves

Farm Aid
https://www.farmaid.org/

Kacey Musgraves Website
http://www.kaceymusgraves.com/

Works Consulted

———. "Kacey Musgraves Competes in Little Miss Tater Tot Pageant." KOKE FM. http://kokefm.com/watch-kacey-musgraves-compete-in-little-miss-tater-tot-pageant/

———. "Kacey Musgraves Comes By Her Artistic Talent Naturally." Universal Music Group Nashville, January 21, 2013. http://pressroom.umgnashville.com/news/kacey-musgraves-comes-by-her-artistic-talent-naturally-audio/

———. "Kacey Musgraves Requests Prayer After Hit & Run Accident Injures Furry Friend." Country Rebel. https://countryrebel.com/blogs/videos/kacey-musgraves-requests-prayer-after-hit-run-accident-injures-furry-friend

Allers, Hannalee. "Kacey Musgraves Says Her Third Album Will Be 'Completely Different.'" The Boot, June 15, 2015. http://theboot.com/kacey-musgraves-third-album/

Allers, Hannahlee. "Kacey Musgraves Explains Inspiration for 'Follow Your Arrow.'" The Boot, October 11, 2013. http://theboot.com/kacey-musgraves-follow-your-arrow/

Bonaguro, Alison. "Kacey Musgraves' Most Prophetic Song is 16 Years Old." CMT, March 5, 2014. http://www.cmt.com/news/1723579/kacey-musgraves-most-prophetic-song-is-16-years-old/

Bonaguro, Alison. "Kacey Musgraves' Secrets of Life on the Bus." CMT, March 7, 2014. http://www.cmt.com/news/1723717/kacey-musgraves-secrets-of-life-on-the-bus/

Brickley, Kelly. "Kacey Musgraves and Others Contribute Voices to 'Hands' for Orlando Tragedy." Sounds Like Nashville, July 6, 2016. http://www.soundslikenashville.com/music/kacey-musgraves-and-others-contribute-voices-to-hands-for-orlando-tragedy/

FURTHER READING

Doyle, Patrick. "Unbreakable Kacey Musgraves: Nashville's Sharpest Rebel Walks the Line." *Rolling Stone*, June 9, 2015. http://www.rollingstone.com/music/news/unbreakable-kacey-musgraves-nashvilles-poppiest-rebel-walks-the-line-20150609

Duffy, Thom. "John Mellencamp, Kacey Musgraves and More on Willie Nelson Making a Difference with 30 Years of Farm Aid." *Billboard*, October 16, 2015. http://www.billboard.com/articles/news/6730162/willie-nelson-farm-aid-john-mellencamp-don-henley-kacey-musgraves-interview

Halperin, Shirley and Chris Willman. "Katy Perry & Kacey Musgraves Take America: Inside Their TV Special, Tour." *Billboard*, May 27, 2014. http://www.billboard.com/articles/columns/pop-shop/6099336/katy-perry-kacey-musgraves-billboard-cover-story-tour-crossroads

Hight, Jewly. "Kacey Musgraves on 'Going Against the Grain,' Country Radio, and Why She's Not Exactly 'Miss Congenial.'" *Billboard*, June 1, 2015. http://www.billboard.com/articles/columns/the-615/6582984/kacey-musgraves-pageant-material-interview-new-music

Hill, Erin. "Grammy Winner Kacey Musgraves: 5 Things to Know about the Country Star." January 27, 2014. https://parade.com/257679/erinhill/grammy-winner-kacey-musgraves-5-things-to-know-about-the-country-star/

Hudak, Josseph. "Kacey Musgraves' 'Follow Your Arrow' Prevails in CMA Song of the Year Race." *Rolling Stone*, November 5, 2014. http://www.rollingstone.com/music/news/kacey-musgraves-follow-your-arrow-cma-song-of-the-year-race-20141105

Hudak, Josseph. "Kacey Musgraves Talks Quirky Christmas Album, New Willie Nelson Duet." *Rolling Stone*, November 18, 2016. http://www.rollingstone.com/country/news/kacey-musgraves-on-christmas-album-new-willie-nelson-duet-w451096

Netemeyer, Sarah. "Meet Kacey Musgraves' New Boyfriend, Ruston Kelly." Country Fancast, October 26, 2016. http://countryfancast.com/meet-kacey-musgraves-boyfriend-ruston-kelly/

Richards, Chris. "Kacey Musgraves, country music's new real deal." *Washington Post*, March 8, 2013. https://www.washingtonpost.com/entertainment/music/kacey-musgraves-country-musics-new-real-deal/2013/03/07/12231970-85c3-11e2-98a3-b3db6b9ac586_story.html

Rotella, Carlo. "Kacey Musgraves's Rebel Twang." *New York Times*, March 15, 2013. http://www.nytimes.com/2013/03/17/magazine/kacey-musgravess-rebel-twang.html

Schalnsky, Evan. "Local Songwriter Trent Dabbs Gets A Boost From ABC's *Nashville*." American Songwriter, October 17, 2012. https://americansongwriter.com/2012/10/local-songwriter-trent-dabbs-gets-a-boost-from-abcs-nashville/

Schwartz, Brie. "Country Superstar Kacey Musgraves Schools Us in How to Be Badass." *Redbook*, June 17, 2015. http://www.redbookmag.com/life/news/a22729/kacey-musgraves/

Stefano, Angela. "Kacey Musgraves, Ruston Kelly Get Engaged on Christmas Eve." The Boot, December 25, 2016. http://theboot.com/kacey-musgraves-ruston-kelly-engaged/

Thiel, Mike. "Hear Zac Brown Band and Kacey Musgraves' John Prine Cover." Taste of Country, April 21, 2017. http://tasteofcountry.com/zac-brown-band-kacey-musgraves-all-the-best/

Thompson, Gayle. "Kacey Musgraves Plans Hometown Charity Concert." The Boot, July 16, 2015. http://theboot.com/kacey-musgraves-hometown-hang-concert-2015/

Thompson, Gayle. "Kacey Musgraves Won't Rush Her Third Album." The Boot, March 21, 2017. http://theboot.com/kacey-musgraves-time-off-2017/

Thompson, Gayle. "'Mama's Broken Heart Was a Reluctant Gift to Miranda Lambert." The Boot, January 30, 2013. http://theboot.com/kacey-musgraves-mamas-broken-heart/

Thompson, Gayle. "Radney Foster Convinced Kacey Musgraves to Move to Nashville." The Boot, January 8, 2014. http://theboot.com/radney-foster-kacey-musgraves-nashville/

Willman, Chris. "Billboard Year in Music 2014: Kacey Musgraves on Singing with Loretta Lynn and Why She No Longer Has a Bucket List." *Billboard*, December 12, 2014. http://www.billboard.com/articles/events/year-in-music-2014/6405602/kacey-musgraves-same-trailer-different-park-number-one-charts-2014

INDEX